**tiger tales**
5 River Road, Suite 128
Wilton, CT 06897
Published in the United States 2021
Originally published in Great Britain
2021 by Little Tiger Press Ltd.

To Riley xx

Text and illustrations by Joanne Partis
Text and illustrations copyright
© 2021 Little Tiger Press Ltd.
ISBN-13: 978-1-68010-258-1
ISBN-10: 1-68010-258-3
Printed in China
LTP/2800/3729/0521

www.tigertalesbooks.com

The Forest Stewardship Council® (FSC®) is an international,
non-governmental organization dedicated to promoting responsible
management of the world's forests. FSC® operates a system of forest
certification and product labeling that allows consumers to identify
wood and wood-based products from well-managed forests.

For more information about the FSC®, please visit their website at www.fsc.org

FSC
www.fsc.org
MIX
Paper from
responsible sources
FSC® C017606

# GOOD NIGHT, TOUCAN

by Joanne Partis

tiger tales

"Ta-da!"

Toucan had decided to throw a
sleepover party for his friends.
"It's going to be **fabulous**," he said.
"I hope everyone can come!"

Everyone was **excited** to receive an invitation.

"A sleepover party? Hooray!"

"Awesome!"

"Party . . . time!"

"Super cool!"

In fact, they were even **more** excited than Toucan had expected.

"Yes, please!" they all cried. "It's going to be the best sleepover **ever!**"

Gulp!

Back at his treetop home, Toucan was starting to worry.
His decorations suddenly didn't feel special enough.
Not for the best sleepover **ever!**

"Not **yummy** enough!"

"Not **snuggly** enough!"

"Ahhh!!"
cried Toucan.
"I need to find things for the
perfect party—now!" he said,
and off he charged into the jungle.

"Fabulous flower decorations!" said Toucan. "Just what I need!"

The little yellow ones were pretty. **O**r the big pink ones?

"I want
the biggest
ones!"

panted Toucan.

He was about to struggle
home when he saw . . .

"Fluffy ferns! What a **snuggly** bed
they would make!" cried Toucan.
He just **had** to have one.

*Whoa!* Toucan thought.
Maybe that was a few too many.

"Huff . . .

puff . . . ," puffed Toucan.

He was furiously flapping to stay above the treetops.
But then he saw something really wonderful!
"Oh, my!" he said. "What a feast those yummy
bananas would make!"

"This sleepover **is** going to be the best after all!" Toucan huffed happily.

Night had fallen in the jungle, and the fireflies were coming out.

"Twinkling lights!" gasped Toucan. "I **must** have them!"

The fireflies darted
here and there.

Toucan swooped · · ·

· · · and then he dove!

Closer and closer, until . . .

"Got you!" he cried. But uh-oh . . . .

Back at Toucan's house, it was sleepover time at last.

But Toucan was nowhere to be seen.

"We're here!" called Monkey.

"It's . . . bed . . . time!" yawned Sloth.

"I brought bedtime stories!" said Tiger.

"Where are you, Toucan?" said Frog.

And **what** was that funny,

dripping sound?

It **was** Toucan!
"Everything is ruined," wailed Toucan.
"It won't be the best sleepover ever!
I don't even have t-t-twinkling lights."

"Yes, you do!" said Frog, pointing up at the stars.

"I love your decorations!" smiled Sloth.

"And I love your berries!" laughed Monkey.

"We have **exactly** what we need to make this sleepover special," said Tiger.

"And

that

is . . ."

"You!" they all cried.
"Oh!" blushed Toucan.
He'd been so silly!

So Toucan snuggled up
with his very best friends
around him.

And that's all he really
needed for the best
sleepover . . . ever!